Jackson's Story

One Dog's Journey to His Forever Home

Elizabeth Baker

Interior Art Credit: Matt Blanchfield

Archway Publishing books may be ordered through booksellers or by contacting:

Archway Publishing
1663 Liberty Drive
Bloomington, IN 47403
www.archwaypublishing.com
1 (888) 242-5904

ISBN: 978-1-4808-5930-2 (sc)
ISBN: 978-1-4808-5929-6 (e)

Print information available on the last page.

Archway Publishing rev. date: 02/09/2018

DEDICATION

To all of the rescue league volunteers who spend countless hours at every stage of the adoption process to ensure that unwanted dogs find their "forever homes": THANK YOU!!

AND to Cecil, the beautiful yellow lab who is the inspiration for this story.

Jackson's Story:
One Dog's Journey to His Forever Home

My name is Jackson. That wasn't always my name - it used to be "Buddy", but a lot has happened to me since then. I'm a dog - I guess a pretty big one, because I've gotten to be taller than most of the other dogs I see. Here is my story:

My First People

My earliest memories are so happy! I loved snuggling up to my mom with my wiggling brothers and sisters. We rolled and tumbled and nipped each other. As we got bigger, people started coming to visit us, and one day a man and a lady and a boy they called "Toby" came to see us. Man and Lady told Toby he could pick out one puppy for his very own. He looked us over carefully, and then picked me up. "Oh,this one! I love this one! This is the one I want!", he said, grinning up at his parents. "His name is Buddy."

Matt

With Toby holding me in his arms, we got into a car. I scrambled to get free and go back to my dog family. I was very scared - I'd never been away from them before - but Toby held me tight, and we drove away. I was trembling with fear and confusion, but Toby was very sweet to me. He stroked me and whispered, "It's OK, Buddy. I'm here". I began to relax a little. Man and Lady talked to Toby as we drove along, telling him that I was *his* dog, and it would be *his* job to take care of me. "Oh, but I LOVE Buddy, and I will ALWAYS take care of him!", Toby promised.

Not Everyone Loves A Puppy

I was just a pup, and I had SO MUCH energy. Sometimes even though we really didn't mean to, Toby and I went a little crazy playing in the house. When that happened, Man or Lady would scold us both and send us outside. But once when we were playing, I knocked over a table, and Man kicked me! I yelped in surprise and hid behind a chair. It hurt my side terribly - no one had ever hurt me before. But it hurt even worse inside - I thought these people liked me! My side was sore for a few days, but my heart was truly broken. All I had ever wanted was to please them.

Sometimes Lady took Toby and me for rides in the car - I loved that! But by now I didn't think Man liked me very much, and he proved it one day when he said to Toby, "This stupid dog is a lot of trouble. You can keep him, but he can't come in the house anymore! And if you don't take care of him, he's going!" So that night I slept outside, alone, tied to a dog house. I was miserable, and I couldn't understand why being a happy, playful pup would get me kicked out of the house. I could tell Toby felt terrible about leaving me all alone at night, and I felt terrible, too!

BUDdY

After a while, I sort of got used to it, but I wasn't really happy, and I feel like doing crazy puppy things anymore. Slowly, the days went by and th another thing happened. A big yellow bus stopped in front of the house, and Toby got on it...and went away. He was gone almost the whole day that day and most days after that, and I was all alone, tied to my dog house with nothing to do. There just wasn't very much fun or love in my life anymore.

Left Out

It seemed that's just how it was now. At least I was fed and had shelter when it rained. Toby was getting bigger, and he had lots of friends now to play with instead of me. Every day I waited hopefully for Toby's big yellow bus to bring him home, but more and more often he wasn't on it. Every time that happened I felt as bad as when I was kicked. Then one night, he forgot to feed me. He was *really* sorry and promised it would NEVER happen again. But only a few days later, it did. Now I was hungry AND lonely. Man yelled at Toby and said "I told you if you didn't take care of that dog, I'd get rid of him, so he's going!" Toby cried and made more promises, but the next day, an awful thing happened. While Toby was away, Man said, "Hey, Buddy - want to go for a ride in the car?" I jumped up and down and wagged my tail, forgetting that Man had never done anything nice with me before. I bounded into the car, and we drove for a long time. When we stopped, Man tied a rope around my neck, and we walked a little way off the road. Then Man tied the other end of the rope to a tree, said "Have a nice life, Buddy", and got back in the car and drove away. "NO", I thought, "Wait! Don't go without me!"

Matt

Abandoned!

If this was a new game, I wasn't at all sure I liked it. But, I thought, maybe Toby was coming to get me. I lay down in the dirt to wait, feeling miserable inside and out. There was some shade from the tree, but it was very hot, and flies kept biting me. I barked and barked and even howled a bit, but Toby didn't come, so I gave up, discouraged. When night came, I tried to sleep, but I was uncomfortable and lonely and very puzzled. I just couldn't understand why people I loved and trusted would do this to me. By morning I was weak from hunger and thirst - I couldn't even stand up for long. After a time, I heard a car, and I pricked up my ears in hope. It didn't sound quite like MY car, though. It drove by and then stopped and backed up. A man and lady I had never seen before got out and walked toward me. I wagged my tail to show them I was friendly. They walked toward me and held out their hands for me to sniff, and I licked their fingers. The lady exclaimed, "Oh, you poor, sweet doggie! Let's get you to the animal shelter!" They untied the rope from the tree, and put me in their car. I was very confused, but these people seemed nice - maybe *they* would take me to Toby.

Soon we stopped outside a building, and the people took me inside. They talked to a man behind a desk, and then handed my rope over to him. Then they turned to leave, and the desk man took me into a big room with cages all along the sides. The cages were all full, and some had more than one dog inside. Desk Man opened a cage that had one dog in it - a dog about my size, and I could tell from sniffing that she was a girl dog. She wagged her tail, so I wagged mine, too, and I knew we were friends.

Matt Blanchfield

There was a water bowl in the cage with dead bugs floating in it, but I was so thirsty I didn't even care. Friend and I lay together quietly waiting...for what? I just hoped Toby would come for me.

Jack and Jill

There were no windows, so we couldn't tell if it was day or night, but some time later Desk Man brought two ladies to our cage. They talked to the man, and I heard words I didn't know like "rescue" and "clinic", and then one of them said, "Yes, we'll take these two with us". So I was leaving again? How would Toby ever find me? - but this time, Friend was coming with me, and that made me feel a little bit better. After another car ride, we arrived at a different building, and the ladies took us inside. This building smelled of all kinds of animals, but it also smelled clean. The person behind the desk asked, "What are their names?" The ladies looked at each other, and one of them said, "We have no idea. They were abandoned with no identification. Let's call them 'Jack' and 'Jill'." Jill and I were taken to side-by-side cages. I was sorry we weren't in the same one, but these cages were clean with clean water bowls, and - best of all - doors that were open to a yard where we could be together and play with other dogs. For the first time in a long time, a little seed of hope began to grow in me.

We lived there for what seemed like a very long time. Everyone was nice to us, and we had walks every day and good food. Someone put something that didn't taste very good on all my fly bites, but it helped them not to itch so much. No matter how nice everyone was, though, I never stopped missing Toby and hoping he'd come to take me home. One day I was taken to a special room where I was given a shot that made me very sleepy. The next thing I remember is waking up back in my cage. I had a sore place between my legs, and my head seemed to be stuck in a bucket. That was annoying, because I really wanted to lick the sore place to make it feel better, but I couldn't get at it with the bucket on my head. I could still go out in the yard and go for walks, but nobody took away the bucket.

Matt

Apparently the same thing happened to Jill, because her head was stuck in a bucket, too! After what seemed like forever, they took my bucket off - what a relief! - and I could lick myself wherever I wanted. Jill's bucket was gone too, so we could play together like we used to.

A Long Trip

And then one day, one of the nice people came to my cage and said "Hey, Jack! You're going for a ride to your forever home!" I had no idea what she meant, but I did know "ride", and given everything that had happened to me lately, I felt a little doubtful. But I wagged my tail anyway - maybe THIS ride would be the ride that would take me back to Toby. Nice Person put me on a leash and took me out to the front of the building where a very big, white trailer truck was parked. It had paw prints painted all over it.

There was an open door on the side of the trailer with a ramp leading up to it. Nice Person handed my leash over to a young man, gave me a quick ear-rub, and said, “Safe travels, Jack.” The young man led me up the ramp and into the truck which was full of cages stacked two-high. Many of the cages had dogs in them already, with little dogs in the upper ones - all of them barking and whining. I was put into one of the larger cages, and then - happily! - Jill was led onto the truck and put in the cage next to mine! I was so glad to see her that I didn’t even mind the noise from the other dogs. A few more dogs were brought on and put in cages, and then the door closed. It was very dark, but nice and cool, and I had Jill right beside me. It was nice to know that I wasn’t alone even though I was completely confused.

The truck stopped twice for more dogs to be led on and put in cages. When it stopped a third time several friendly, happy people came and took us, a few at a time, out into the sunlight for a short walk so we could pee. They even gave us a little water and a snack before returning us to our cages on the truck. A few new dogs joined us, and we were off again. We drove for what seemed like a very long time, and the next time we stopped and the door was opened, it was dark outside. More nice people walked and fed us as before, and then the young man who first took me to my cage climbed in with his sleeping bag. He petted as many of us as he could reach and talked to us softly before he curled up in his sleeping bag and went to sleep. It felt so good to have a friendly person there!

Matt Blanchfield

In the morning, after a little snack, we drove on for awhile, and then stopped. This time, several dogs were led out of the truck. I couldn't see what was happening outside, but I could hear a lot of happy cheering, and that was the last we saw of those dogs. But the next time we stopped, something terrible happened! Jill was one of the dogs led out into the cheering crowd! I barked frantically and scratched at the door of my cage and even howled! But she was gone. Oh, Jill - you were the one thing that made me happy when I was so lonely and confused, and now you're gone, too. I laid my head on my paws and didn't move for the rest of that long ride.

Matt Blanchfield

I had never felt so much pain and sadness in my life! Everything that had ever made me happy was gone - Toby, Jill, my home - and now here I was in a cage in a dark truck - oh, *WHY* was this happening!?

Forever

I felt so hopeless that I didn't even notice when the truck stopped again. Then suddenly I was aware of light pouring in through the door along with fresh, cool air, and I could hear cheering crowds again. I hoped we'd come back for Jill. But the nice young man who had slept with us last night opened the door to my cage and attached a leash to my collar. "Come on, Jack, let's go meet your forever family", he said. He led me to the door and down the ramp, and there, at the bottom, a lady squatted down with her arms outstretched. A smiling man was behind her. When I reached the bottom of the ramp, the lady threw her arms around me in a big hug and cried, "Welcome, Jackson, we're so happy you're here!!

Matt Blanchfield

The young man from the truck handed my leash over to Smiling Man. I was so anxious to pee that I didn't really greet them. They walked me over to a grassy place so I could relieve myself, and they gave me a fresh drink of water. I looked and looked, but there was no sign of Jill - there wasn't anybody familiar. But these people were very nice, and they really seemed to like me! They led me to a car and said, Come on, Jackson, let's go home!". *Jackson?* Well, people had been calling me "Jack" for a while, and "Jackson" was pretty close, so I guessed that would be OK.

This car ride was very different from the long ride in a dark truck. I was allowed to lie on the comfortable back seat or sit up and look out the windows, and every so often the lady would hand me a small treat! Once in a while I stuck my head over the front seat and nuzzled one of them in the neck to say "thank you". Finally, we stopped beside a house, and they took me inside and took my leash off. "Welcome to your forever home, Jackson!" the lady said. I was excited and a little nervous, but I actually started to feel something like hope. I rushed around from room to room sniffing everything. Then they let me outside into a huge grassy yard with a fence around it - and no dog house in sight! Back inside, they showed me where my water and food bowls were, and gave me my supper. I realized I was starving - I hadn't had a real meal since before the truck ride. After I ate, the man took me out to the yard and tossed a ball for me to fetch. I just love to chase anything that moves fast, so I ran after the ball and picked it up, but I didn't quite know what to do with it after that. The man laughed and called me back, and pretty soon I caught on! That night, when they went upstairs, they invited me to come, too. They showed me a nice, soft bed - right next to their bed!! - and that's where I was to sleep. As I started to fall asleep, almost like in a happy dream, I felt the man's hand on my head, and I heard him say, *"Good boy, Jackson."*

Today I'm a happy dog.

Matt
Blandfield

I think of these people as Mom and Dad now, and I think of myself as Jackson, although once in a while someone will call me "Buddy" (I wonder how they know???). Mom and Dad take me for walks every day, and always we go back to the house, so I know now that this is HOME!

I think there will always be things that bring back painful memories of the awful times and how hopeless and confused I was. Whenever we're on a walk and a car passes by, I stare after it wondering if that's the car that left me behind and I get that terrible left-behind feeling all over again. Mom and Dad take me for lots of car rides, and I still love to go, but at first I didn't want to get out at the end of the ride just in case they planned to tie me to a tree and leave me. I'm learning, though, that we ALWAYS come back home, and now I can trust them. I'm still hoping I'll find Toby, and whenever I see a boy I want to go to him just in case it's him. I miss Jill, too. I still hurt inside from being so misunderstood and mistreated and abandoned. But Mom and Dad seem to understand, and they don't mind that in the house I have to keep one of them in sight at all times, so I follow them wherever they go...even to the bathroom! It's hard for me to believe that they won't ever leave me. I'm learning that it's okay to be a puppy, and when I act silly and bouncy, Mom and Dad just laugh. I was worried the first time I knocked something over that I might be kicked, but they just said "Oh, Jackson, you silly pup!" and gave me hugs! Now, every day is full of adventures and exercise and treats and LOVE. I hope it's like this FOREVER!

Afterword - How You Can help

Sadly, this story, or one very much like it, could be told by any one of *hundreds* of dogs who are rescued from overcrowded shelters in the South and transported to the northeast for adoption *every week*. Someone taking a dog to an animal shelter usually has to pay a fee, so many people choose to abandon their pets (as Jackson was) instead. But why are there so *many* homeless dogs in the South? One reason is that their owners do not neuter them (fix them so they can't make puppies). **Here are some ways you can help:**

1. Know that dogs feel pain (inside and out), and fear and confusion and sadness - just like you! Your dog wants to please you - he loves and trusts you. ALWAYS be kind to him.
2. Neuter your dog (or urge your parents to). This does not change the dog's enjoyment of life - it just keeps unwanted puppies from being born. Veterinarians will sometimes offer free or low-cost neutering clinics.
3. If you or someone you know decides to give up a dog, remember that most dog rescue groups will take in an unwanted dog free of charge and with no questions asked. Google "dog rescue leagues". DO NOT abandon your dog!!!

CPSIA information can be obtained
at www.ICGtesting.com
Printed in the USA
BVHW02s0601010518
514883BV00011B/47/P

9 781480 859302